™

THE MOVIE STORYBOOK

UNIVERSAL PICTURES AND STUDIOCANAL PRESENT A WORKING TITLE PRODUCTION A JONATHAN FRAKES FILM "THUNDERBIRDS" BILL PAXTON ANTHONY EDWARDS SOPHIA MYLES AND BEN KINGSLEY CASTING BY MARY SELWAY CDG FIONA WEIR MUSIC BY HANS ZIMMER COSTUME DESIGNER MARIT ALLEN EDITOR MARTIN WALSH ACE PRODUCTION DESIGNER JOHN BEARD DIRECTOR OF PHOTOGRAPHY BRENDAN GALVIN EXECUTIVE PRODUCERS DEBRA HAYWARD LIZA CHASIN PRODUCED BY TIM BEVAN ERIC FELLNER MARK HUFFAM STORY BY PETER HEWITT AND WILLIAM OSBORNE SCREENPLAY BY WILLIAM OSBORNE AND MICHAEL McCULLERS

STUDIO CANAL WORKING TITLE PG PARENTAL GUIDANCE SUGGESTED SOME MATERIAL MAY NOT BE SUITABLE FOR CHILDREN INTENSE ACTION SEQUENCES AND LANGUAGE dts SDDS DOLBY DIGITAL DIRECTED BY JONATHAN FRAKES www.thunderbirdsmovie.com A UNIVERSAL RELEASE UNIVERSAL © 2004 UNIVERSAL STUDIOS ® For rating reasons, go to www.filmratings.com

THUNDERBIRDS: THE MOVIE STORYBOOK

First published in the USA by HarperFestival in 2004
First published in Great Britain by HarperCollins*Entertainment* 2004
HarperCollins*Entertainment* is an imprint of HarperCollins Publishers Ltd,
77-85 Fulham Palace Road, Hammersmith, London W6 8JB

0-00-717806-9

1 3 5 7 9 8 6 4 2

www.harpercollinschildrensbooks.co.uk

Printed and bound in the UK

THE MOVIE STORYBOOK

Adapted by Kate Egan

Based on a motion picture screenplay
by William Osborne and Michael McCullers

Story by Peter Hewitt and William Osborne

Based on the original television series "Thunderbirds" © ITC Distribution, LLC

HarperCollins*Entertainment*
An Imprint of HarperCollins*Publishers*

Alan Tracy was riveted to the TV screen along with his classmates at boarding school. They were watching the world-famous Thunderbirds make a dramatic rescue after a major accident on an oil rig.

None of his classmates knew it, but Alan's dad, Jeff Tracy, was the head of the top secret organization called International Rescue, and it was him they were watching on TV. With his high-tech equipment, Jeff Tracy and his team rescued people from all kinds of disasters. Everyone called them the Thunderbirds, after their incredible rescue vehicles.

Alan's older brothers were Thunderbirds already, and Alan was deter-mined to follow in their footsteps. But Alan's brothers teased him about the schools that had kicked him out, and Alan's dad still treated him like a little kid. Sometimes Alan wondered if they'd ever take him seriously.

For spring break, Alan was going home to Tracy Island, the Thunderbirds' tropical hideaway. The Thunderbirds' London secret agent, Lady Penelope, came to pick him up in her pink limousine, called *FAB 1*. Alan barely spoke on the way home. He just kept wondering when he'd be able to show his family what he was made of.

On his first night home, Alan and his best friend, Fermat, sneaked into the storage bay where the powerful Thunderbird vehicles were kept. *Thunderbird 1*, the fastest ship in the fleet, had just returned from a mission. The boys sat in the flight deck and pretended to prepare for takeoff. "Okay, Fermat, run preflight checks!" Alan ordered. "Commence main engine sequence."

Fermat grinned, replying, "F.A.B., Alan." That's what real Thunderbirds always said.

As usual, though, Alan got carried away. He couldn't resist flipping a switch—and it turned on every panel in the cockpit. Jeff Tracy's stern face appeared on the ship's main monitor. "My office, right now," said his father. The boys were busted—and their vacation had barely begun.

Alan's punishment felt like the end of the world to him. But he didn't know that a bigger problem was lurking in a submarine close to shore. There, a villain called The Hood was putting the finishing touches on his scheme to ruin the Thunderbirds forever.

The Hood was about to send the Tracys to a decoy disaster in space—and trap them there! Then The Hood would sneak onto the Tracys' island and steal their rescue vehicles. He planned to use them to break into banks around the world! The Thunderbirds would no longer be famous for their daring rescues but for their heartless crimes. It was a simple plan. But The Hood didn't count on one thing: the teamwork of Alan, Fermat, and their friend, Tin-Tin, the daughter of Jeff Tracy's loyal employee Kyrano.

Alan stood on the beach with Tin-Tin and Fermat, sulking as *Thunderbird 3* soared overhead. Alan figured his family was leaving him behind for yet another rescue mission. He had no idea that this operation might be their last. But he knew something was wrong when a submarine rose out of the water. Security had been breached—and his family was far away!

The friends had to find a way to sneak back into the Tracy home fast. Together they crept through the ventilation system toward the command center run by Fermat's dad, Brains. Maybe he could help them. But the kids were too late. The Hood controlled everything now, even the ship that Jeff Tracy had just piloted away. And Brains had been taken prisoner!

Alan and his friends didn't want to be next. When The Hood spotted them, the kids leaped down a launch chute into the silo where *Thunderbird 2* was stored. Alan headed for the amazing vehicles inside the equipment pods. Fermat shouted, "Those are only to be used in emergencies!" Alan glared at him. This *was* an emergency. They were the only ones who could save the Thunderbirds, and they'd have to do whatever it took. But first they had to lose The Hood.

Fermat fumbled at the wheel of the *Firefly*, an eight-wheeled truck with a cannon on top. While he steered, Tin-Tin blasted The Hood's goons with a flood of fire-retardant foam!

Then Alan blew a hole in the wall with the powerful cannon at the front of the *Thunderizer*! The kids had only seconds to escape. Alan wished Fermat would move a little faster, but somehow they made it out alive.

They thought they were safe sliding down a different vent . . . until The Hood ordered his minions to fire a rocket! Alan, Tin-Tin, and Fermat flew into the Pacific Ocean seconds ahead of a huge fireball!

Now what? Alan wondered. He wished Fermat would stop complaining. It wasn't his fault that Fermat didn't know how to swim. He had to give his friend some credit, though. Fermat had stolen the guidance processor for *Thunderbird 2* when they were in the silo. The Hood couldn't take off without it.

Fermat also had a plan. If they got to the island's satellite station, they could reach Alan's family in space—and help them come back to earth. Tin-Tin was the only one who knew the way to the station, though. "We have to go through the jungle," she announced. "It's going to be dangerous."

The kids looked at each other until Alan broke the silence, saying, "I'm in!" Alan was always up for an adventure.

Meanwhile, the other Tracys were struggling. *Thunderbird 5*, their spacecraft, had been damaged beyond repair. And The Hood controlled the systems that would have allowed them to escape in *Thunderbird 3*. Time and oxygen were running out.

The kids braved rough terrain on the way to the satellite station. Alan helped Fermat keep up when he started to fall behind.

Once the work began, though, he became impatient. Alan pestered Fermat until his friend said, "Don't rush me!" Just then there was a bright flash and a puff of smoke. The equipment was broken. As usual, it was all Alan's fault.

Fermat finally got it running again. He made contact with *Thunderbird 5*! Alan's dad gasped, "Follow emergency procedure! Wait for Lady Penelope at the rendezvous point!" But The Hood jammed the transmission before he could say anything else. The Tracys were in graver danger than ever. And, even worse, now The Hood knew where Alan, Fermat, and Tin-Tin were!

Soon some of The Hood's men appeared in a monstrous beach buggy.

Alan and his friends ducked into a junkyard. There they found the pieces of an old hoversled and began to fix it up.

Fermat and Tin-Tin weren't sure it would work. When Alan added a passenger car to the back of the sled, Fermat said, "That's going to make this harder to control."

When Alan was ready to go, Fermat stood firm. "I don't think it's safe," he announced. "And if we're a team, we should make decisions as a team." Tin-Tin totally agreed.

Alan was fed up. "You don't think anything is safe," he retorted angrily. "Do you want to take a vote, or do you want to get out of here?" Then he hopped onto the sled. Fermat and Tin-Tin were angry, but they had to follow.

Together the kids zigzagged down a mountain. Alan pushed the sled to go faster and faster as the beach buggy gained on them.

Fermat screamed, "You're going too fast!"

Alan paid no attention. He was too busy trying to steer through a narrow space between two rocks. He made it, barely.

It's lucky I'm not afraid to take risks, Alan thought. Where would his friends be without him? He turned around coolly. "What did I tell you?" he said to them. But Fermat and Tin-Tin were gone!

Now Alan wondered where *he* would be without his friends! He was afraid he knew the answer: nowhere. Fermat's dad, Brains, and Tin-Tin's dad, Kyrano, helped Jeff Tracy keep the *Thunderbirds* flying. Suddenly Alan realized he couldn't work alone any more than his dad could. He needed Fermat's brains. He needed Tin-Tin's courage. He needed help! Alan would have to find his friends before he did anything else.

Alan darted through the woods around his family's house. He suspected The Hood would be there—so his friends couldn't be far away. Alan was surprised to see Lady Penelope battling The Hood one-on-one. She was an amazing fighter, but she was no match for The Hood. He was an expert in martial arts and a master of mind control.

Soon enough The Hood turned his attention to Alan. "You have some-thing that belongs to me," he said in a creepy voice. Then he took the guidance processor back with his supernatural powers!

The Hood pocketed the processor and threw Alan into a giant freezer. Alan's friends were already there! So were Tin-Tin and Fermat's parents and Lady Penelope. Everyone's lips were turning blue. But Lady Penelope wasn't about to let them freeze. She kicked off one of her high-heeled shoes and aimed it at an icicle. When it fell, the icicle cut through the ropes that bound her driver, Parker, and soon he freed everyone else!

Fermat's dad raced to the control room and worked furiously at the keyboard. But it was Fermat who hacked into the system and finally got access. Now he waited for someone on the ship to respond. Onboard, the Tracys were almost unconscious. But at last Alan's dad spoke up. Fermat restored their power immediately. They were going to be okay.

Alan was proud of his friend, but he figured Fermat was still furious with him. As usual, Alan had underestimated him. Fermat just said, "We make quite a pair. It's hard for me to talk and hard for you to listen." He didn't need to say any more—Alan was forgiven. And now they were on a mission!

The Hood was nearing his first target, London, and the Tracys, aboard *Thunderbird 5*, were too far out in space to stop him. "Let me go after him!" Alan begged his dad. "He'll destroy everything the Thunderbirds stand for!" He didn't expect his dad to actually let him, though. Jeff Tracy usually didn't trust Alan with big responsibilities.

But maybe things had changed. Without Alan, Jeff Tracy would have been lost in space. Without Alan, the Thunderbirds would be destroyed already. To Alan's surprise, his dad said, "We'll meet you there, son. Thunderbirds are *go*!"

Alan said, "I can do this. I know I can." Then he stopped. He looked at Fermat and Tin-Tin. "What am I saying?" he added. "*We* can do this!"

The boys climbed into the pilots' seats in *Thunderbird 1*, just as they had at the beginning of spring break. This time it was for real! Alan said, "Fermat, main engine start." Naturally Fermat replied, "F.A.B." They swooped in to the center of London—just as The Hood arrived in *Thunderbird 2*.

The Hood was being reckless. What did he care if he crushed bystanders on the ground? Everyone would think it was the Thunderbirds! He felt the same way when his crew burrowed underground in the *Mole*, a huge drilling vehicle stored in *Thunderbird 2*. So what if he hit the supports for the monorail track? The Hood wasn't in the rescue business. He just wanted to rob banks.

Alan and his friends wanted to go after The Hood right away. But no true Thunderbird could let the monorail's passengers get hurt! The kids took back *Thunderbird 2* easily. Then they fired a missile which trailed a cable. The cable wound around the support for the track and kept it from breaking.

But only for a minute! Alan did his best, but the monorail's track still cracked in half. The car slid right into the river Thames!

The kids were discouraged, but they couldn't give up. Alan decided it was time to use *Thunderbird 4*. He went down in the bright-yellow submarine. If *Thunderbird 4* could be connected to *Thunderbird 2*, everyone would be fine. But Fermat realized he couldn't fire another cable without endangering the passengers. Luckily Tin-Tin volunteered for a dangerous job. She dove into the river, swam beneath the submarine, and attached the cable by hand!

Alan lowered *Thunderbird 4*'s robot arms onto the submerged car. One by one they grabbed it. Then a metal probe cut through the twisted metal to free the car from the track. Next, Fermat maneuvered *Thunderbird 2* to pluck *Thunderbird 4*—and the monorail car—out of the water at last!

The rescue completed, there was just one thing left to do: find The Hood and stop him once and for all. The other Tracys arrived just in time to help. Alan couldn't help being a little cocky. "Glad you could join us, Dad," he said. Jeff Tracy smiled. He was proud of his youngest son.

Alan's dad led the way into the bank vault. But he was ambushed by The Hood's crew. Alan would have to face The Hood alone! The Hood was heading toward the *Mole*, so Alan climbed its teeth to get within striking distance. Then The Hood turned the drill on! Its teeth moved faster and faster. Alan was about to be eaten up.

The Hood slipped! Now he was in the *Mole*'s mouth and Alan stood above him! After all he'd been through, Alan wanted him dead. But he also knew what was expected of the Thunderbirds. Alan snatched The Hood's wrist before the villain could fall to his death. "I don't want to save your life," Alan said, sighing. "But it's what we do."

Alan had stopped The Hood. He'd saved his family's lives—and lived up to their lofty goals. He'd learned a thing or two about his friends and himself. But the best reward was this: Alan Tracy was a Thunderbird at last.